EMERGENCY Chopper

Dear Reader

In this book you will find out about real-life emergency choppers. You will read about rescues that save people's lives.

YOU NEVER KNOW WHEN YOU'LL FIND YOURSELF WINCHING SOMEONE OFF THE SIDE OF A MOUNTAIN.

You'll also find out about the invention of helicopters on page 4. On page 5, there's the story of the 14-year-old boy who flew helicopters and broke many records in the USA.

I hope you enjoy reading about emergency choppers and their work as much as I enjoyed writing about them!

John Parsons

My sincere thanks to the following people for their time, information, images and enthusiasm for this book:

Quentin and Wayne, from the helicopter rescue organisation in Christchurch, New Zealand.

NELSON
CENGAGE Learning™
For learning solutions, visit cengage.com.au

Contents

EMERGENCY Chopper

3 An Emergency Procedure

Quentin explains what happens during an emergency. Every minute counts when you are saving someone's life.

4 An Emergency Paramedic

Wayne is a paramedic. His job is to help save lives in helicopter emergencies. Wayne works in road ambulances, too.

5 A Real-Life Emergency Call-Out

Quentin and Wayne are called out to a real-life emergency … in the middle of the author's information report!

HISTORY FEATURE

Helicopter Flight Firsts

The first piloted helicopter was invented in 1907, but its flight was not successful. By 1940, the first successful helicopter was invented by Igor Sikorsky.

HELICOPTER

"Helicopter" is made up of two words: "helico" (which means spiral) and "pter" (which means wings).

Igor's Story

As a ten-year-old boy, Igor built planes out of paper and bamboo. He also built a toy helicopter with paper blades and thin pieces of rubber.

In 1908, he read about Orville and Wilbur Wright and their success flying the first plane. Then he decided to study flight.

Igor Sikorsky (1889–1972)

Helicopter Firsts for Igor

In 1941, Igor's helicopters won all the world records for helicopter flight.

In 1958, Igor's company invented the world's first helicopter that could land and take off from water.

Social Studies and History

Young Helicopter Pilot Breaks Records

In 2006 in the USA, 14-year-old Jonathan Strickland became the youngest person to:

- fly a helicopter solo
- fly a helicopter and an aeroplane solo on the same day
- fly a helicopter internationally (from the USA to Canada and back).

Jonathan Strickland

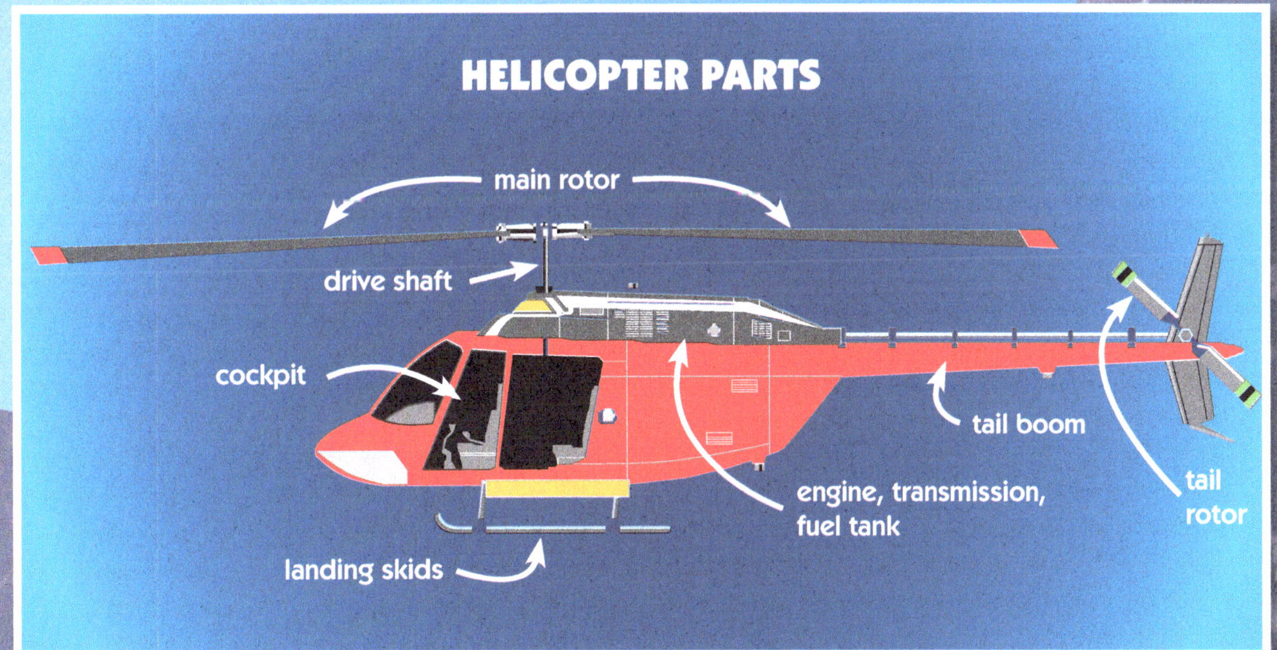

1 An Emergency Rescue

A Flying Ambulance Comes!

This flying ambulance has no sirens. There are no flashing lights or blaring horns. Yet it speeds towards an emergency at over 220 kilometres per hour.

Rotors Roar

Instead of a siren, there is the sound of helicopter rotors. They slash through the air at hundreds of revolutions per minute.

The roar of the engines and the pulse of the rotors make the air vibrate. This seems to increase as they begin to drop towards the rescue site.

"Hotel Juliet Charlie, over"

Ready for Action

Inside, the emergency paramedics crouch, ready for action.

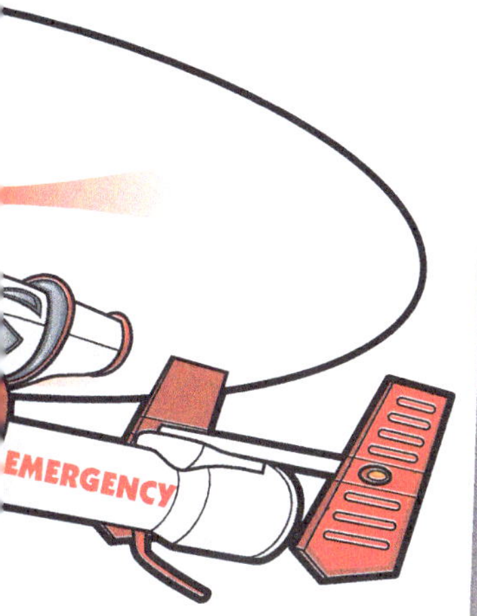

With barely a bump, the pilot lands this very heavy helicopter. It's another emergency, another day, and another mission for "Hotel Juliet Charlie". That's the call sign for this life-saving helicopter.

Language and Communication

ABC: Alpha, Bravo, Charlie Alphabet

Many people spell out words over the phone or by radio, using the NATO Phonetic Alphabet. For example, if someone says they live in "Smyth Street", it may sound like "Smith Street". But no mistakes can be made if it is spelt out:

"Sierra" for "s", "Mike" for "m", "Yankee" for "y", "Tango" for "t", "Hotel" for "h".

The NATO Phonetic Alphabet

A: Alpha	N: November
B: Bravo	O: Oscar
C: Charlie	P: Papa
D: Delta	Q: Quebec
E: Echo	R: Romeo
F: Foxtrot	S: Sierra
G: Golf	T: Tango
H: Hotel	U: Uniform
I: India	V: Victor
J: Juliet	W: Whisky
K: Kilo	X: X-ray
L: Lima	Y: Yankee
M: Mike	Z: Zulu

pilots communicating by radio

2 An Emergency Pilot

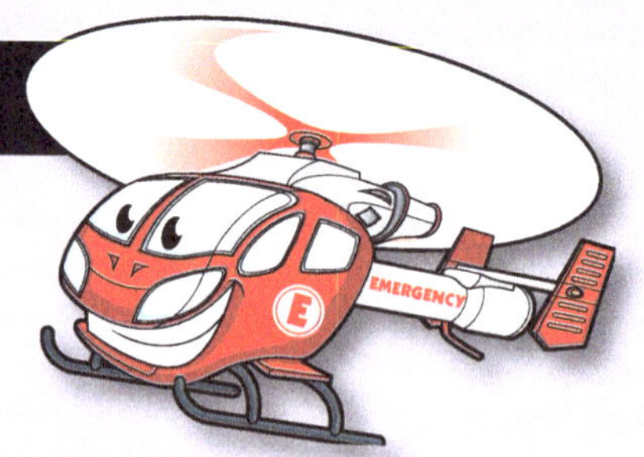

The Author Meets **Quentin**

I met the emergency helicopter pilot of "Hotel Juliet Charlie", Quentin. He works from a helicopter base in New Zealand. He has been flying helicopters for 20 years.

As a child, Quentin was interested in flying aircraft. But then he got a weekend job working with helicopters. He knew that was what he wanted to do.

Quentin

In Training

First, Quentin trained as an aeroplane pilot. Then he learnt how to fly helicopters.

"They're quite different from planes to fly," explains Quentin. He had to fly helicopters for 150 hours before he got his helicopter licence.

the dials in a helicopter cockpit

An Experienced Pilot

Now, Quentin is an experienced pilot. He is able to fly his emergency helicopter into difficult and dangerous places. He can go where people need to be rescued or helped.

Technology

Warning Technology

New technology warns helicopter ambulances if they fly close to obstacles, such as mountains or tall antennas.

a helicopter flying near mountains

A helicopter pilot must concentrate on many instruments at once.

A Variety of Jobs

"There's a lot of variety in my job," Quentin says. "Every day is different for an emergency helicopter pilot."

"You never know when you'll find yourself winching someone off the side of a mountain in blowing winds and pelting rain."

QUENTIN

Safety First

Quentin always puts safety first. He decides whether it is safe to complete each rescue. He knows that people's lives depend on him.

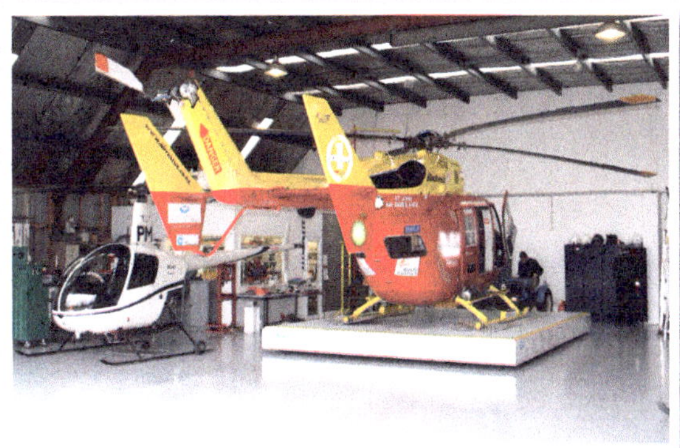
inside a helicopter hangar

Quentin always does everything he can to fly safely to the rescue site. The lives of the patients and the paramedics on board depend on his skills as a pilot.

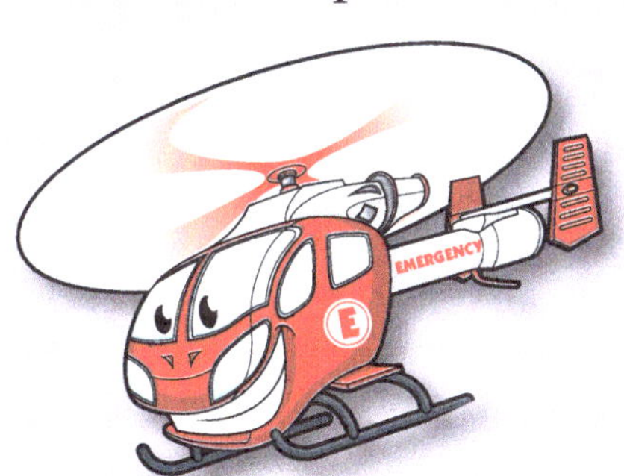

a helipad caution sign

Social Studies

Helpful Helicopters

Helicopters have many uses, such as air-sea rescues, firefighting, traffic control, carrying supplies to oil rigs at sea, and for travel to and from work.

In some situations, helicopters are safer to use than planes because:

- Helicopters can cope better in some bad weather.
- Helicopters can reach difficult areas more easily.
- A pilot can slow down, stop or fly backwards and sideways.

3 An Emergency Procedure

Every **Minute** Counts!

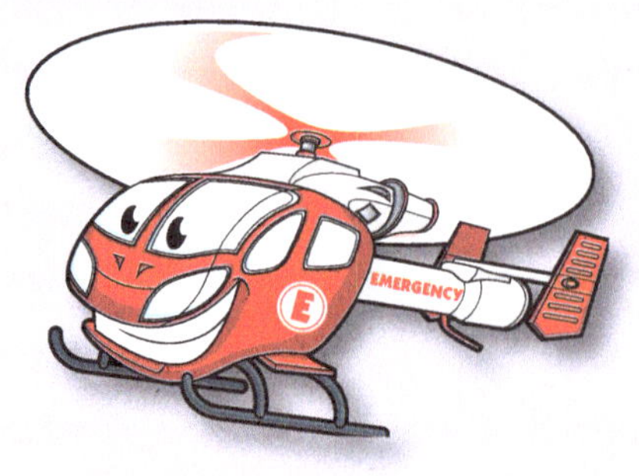

When people are seriously injured, every minute counts.

People can be injured in places far from roads. A regular ambulance may not be able to reach the injured person.

They may have fallen down a cliff or a mountainside. Also, people may be stranded in remote bush or snowfields.

a snowfields rescue

Emergency Alert

What happens when people need to be rescued by helicopter?

First, the police receive information about an accident. Then an emergency alert goes to the ambulance communications centre. They send an urgent message to the helicopter pilot's special pager. They cary their pagers with them at all times.

Police receive information about an accident

↓

Police alert ambulance centre

↓

The ambulance centre pages helicopter pilot

↓

The rescue helicopter responds

Social Studies

Royal Flying Doctors

The Royal Flying Doctor Service of Australia helps people who live in remote areas. It provides doctors and emergency medical help. This charity can fly a doctor to a patient, or the patient to hospital or a clinic, which is usually far away.

a Royal Flying Doctor aircraft

Quentin checks his helicopter.

Safety Checks

Early each morning Quentin checks the helicopter. He can then be sure that it is safe and ready to fly at any time.

Health and Social Studies

Safety Around Helicopters

There are many things to remember if you want to stay safe around helicopters:

- stay well clear of a helicopter as it takes off or lands
- protect your eyes when a helicopter takes off or lands – the rotor blades can swirl up dust and small objects
- keep your head down when you are near the helicopter
- approach a helicopter from the front so the pilot can see you – never approach a helicopter from behind
- hold on tight to any light things such as hats – it's dangerous if anything hits the moving rotor blades.

Stay clear!

Emergency Air Space

The helicopter base is near an airport. When Quentin has to go, he must radio the air traffic control tower. There's no time to waste!

The air traffic controllers know Quentin's call sign – "Hotel Juliet Charlie". When they hear that, they know there is an emergency. They keep the airspace over the airport clear, so that Quentin can take off safely.

an air traffic control tower

an air traffic controller

4 An Emergency Paramedic

A **Paramedic** Helps

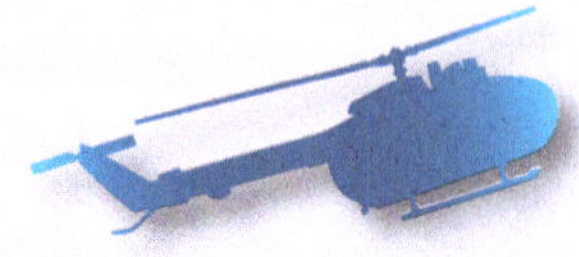

Wayne, a paramedic

The rescue helicopter can carry one or two paramedics. They help with the rescue.

Paramedics treat the injured patient on the flight to the hospital.

An Advanced Paramedic

In the helicopter hangar, Quentin introduces me to Wayne. Wayne is an advanced paramedic, which means that he is very experienced.

"I started working in road ambulances," says Wayne. "Now I do four days of helicopter work and then I have some days off. Then I do four days of road ambulance work."

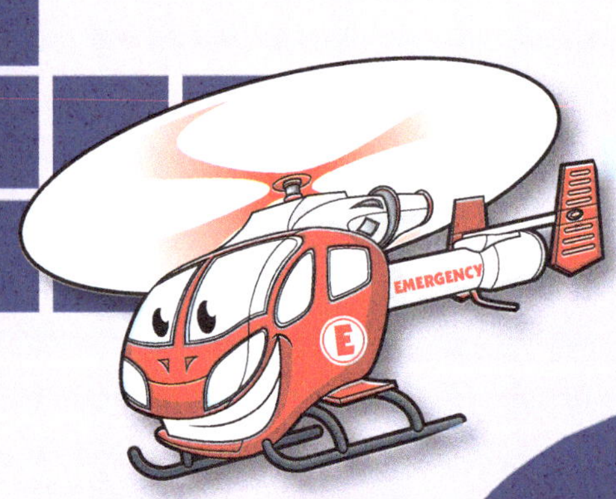

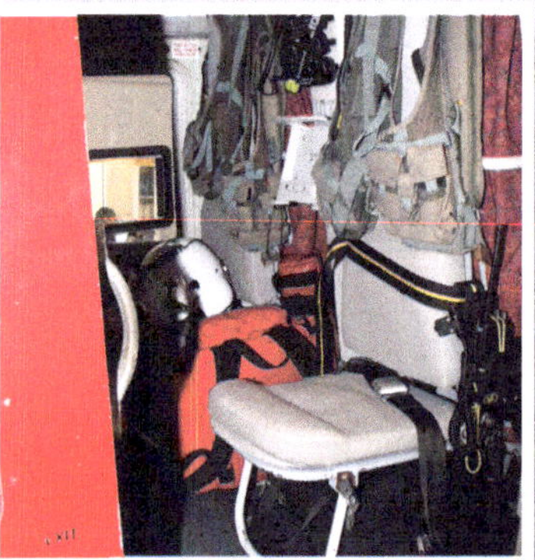
the paramedic's seat

The Paramedic's Equipment

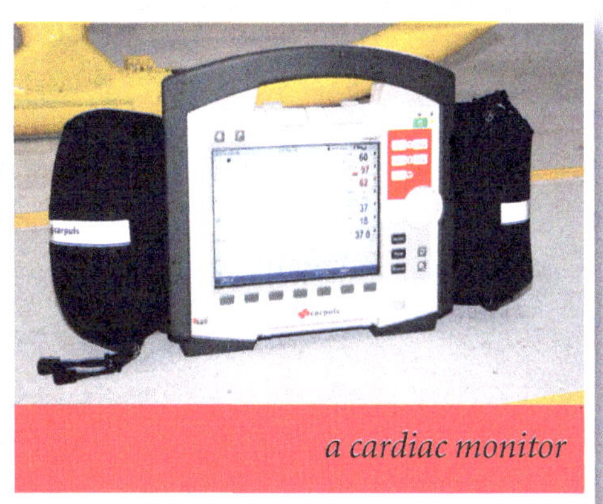
a cardiac monitor

The paramedics' equipment is kept ready for a quick response. They know that accidents and emergencies can happen at any time. They must be prepared for action.

Wayne says that the emergency helicopter is well equipped. It has all the things that a normal "road" ambulance would have.

A Heart Monitor Onboard

Wayne shows me a special cardiac monitor on the helicopter. "This gives us information about a patient's heart," he says. "We can send this information to the hospital while we are still flying. That means the emergency team at the hospital are prepared. They have valuable information about the patient before we arrive. It saves a lot of time."

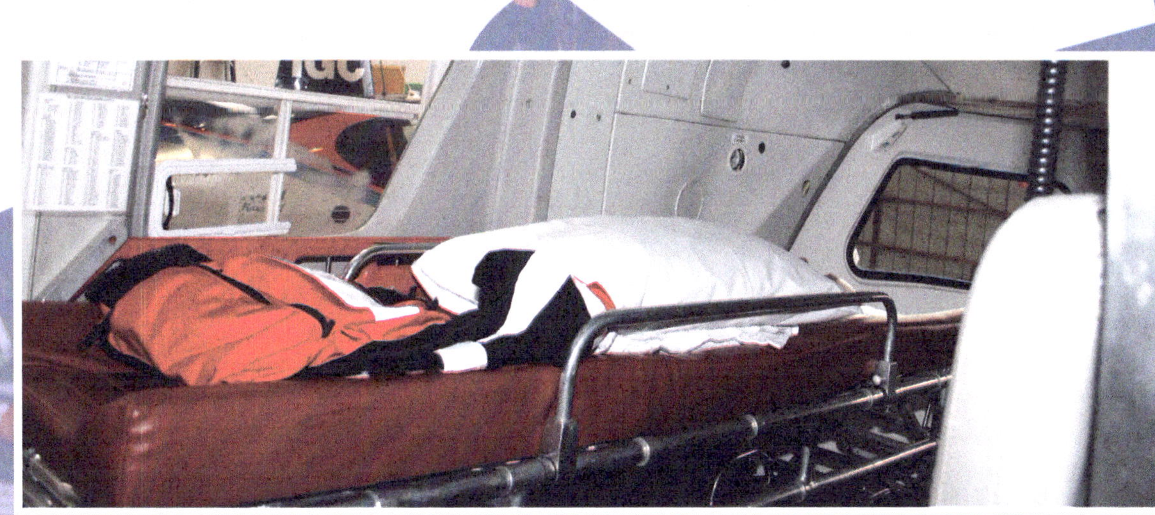
The inside of the helicopter is kept ready for patients.

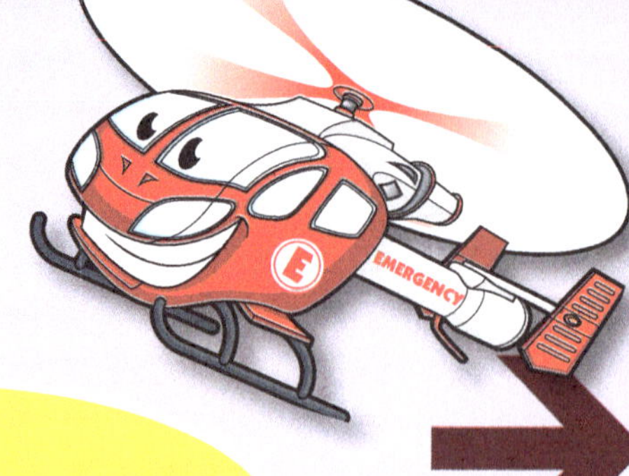

Q: "If someone wants to be an emergency helicopter paramedic, is there a lot of competition?"

A: Wayne laughs. "It's not for everyone," he says.

Wayne

"NOT EVERYONE WANTS TO BE HANGING OFF A HELICOPTER, BEING WINCHED DOWN FROM HIGH ABOVE THE GROUND!

WAYNE"

A REAL Emergency Interrupts!

I'm about to ask Wayne another question. Suddenly we hear a beeping sound. He stops laughing. A serious look crosses his face.

Wayne and Quentin quickly check their pagers.

"Got to go," says Wayne. Quentin calls out the place they need to go to. Both men quickly, but calmly, leave the helicopter hangar.

This is no practise drill. This is a real emergency!

a rescue helicopter on the way to a dangerous sea rescue

5 A Real-Life Emergency Call-Out

Got to **GO NOW!**

Seconds after the alert, a tractor pushes the helicopter out of the hangar.

Quentin grabs his red flight suit from the pilot's seat, and races inside to change.

When the helicopter stops, both Quentin and Wayne prepare the helicopter for its emergency mission.

Wayne makes a final check of the life-saving equipment he will need.

ready to roll

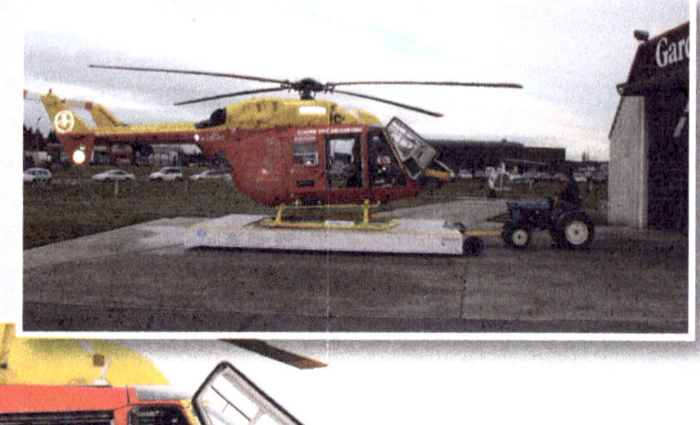

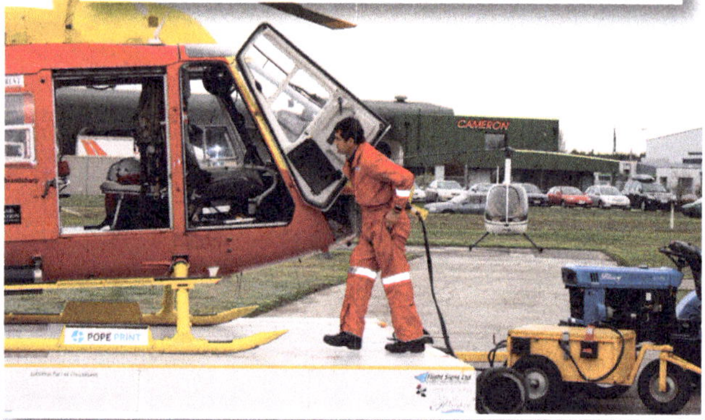

The tractor pushes the helicopter out for take-off.

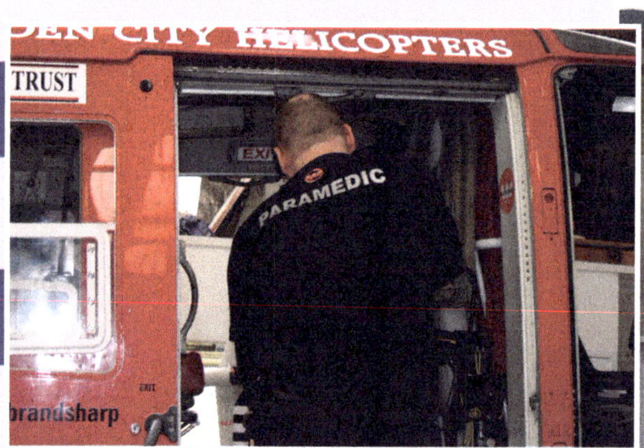

Wayne getting ready for the rescue flight

Quentin with his flight suit

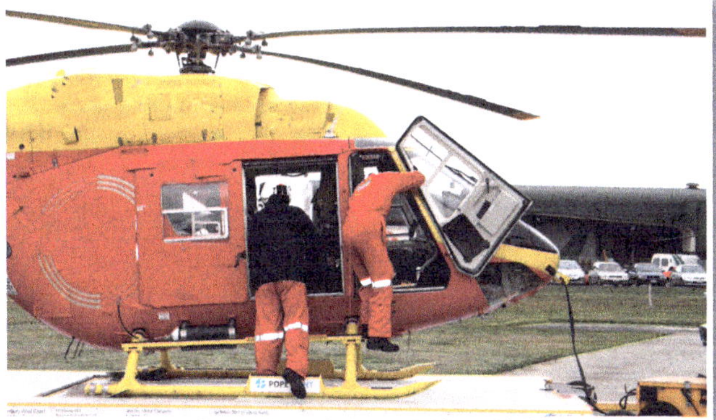

Quentin and Wayne climb aboard.

Ready to Leave

Quentin waves to me.

"Sorry we had to cut short our chat," he says.

"No problem," I call back. "Have a safe flight!"

Quentin climbs into the pilot's seat. He starts the twin jet engines that power the helicopter.

The rotor blades above the aircraft start to rotate. At the rear of the helicopter, the tail rotor spins.

Quentin and Wayne check all systems.

final check

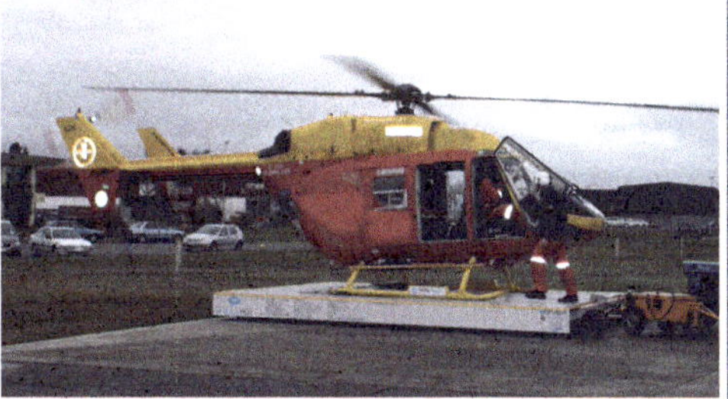

Start the engines!

Safe to Fly

The crew put their helmets on. Then they can hear each other above the noise of the powerful engines.

When they know they're ready to fly, they shut the doors and strap themselves in.

Quentin makes an emergency call to the air traffic control tower at the airport. He gets permission to take off straight away.

calling air traffic control

On the Way

Suddenly, the noise increases. There is a deep roar as Quentin opens the throttle on the helicopter's engines.

The rotors bite into the surrounding air at top speed. A powerful gust of wind sweeps around the take-off area.

Suddenly, the helicopter is airborne.

doors are closed

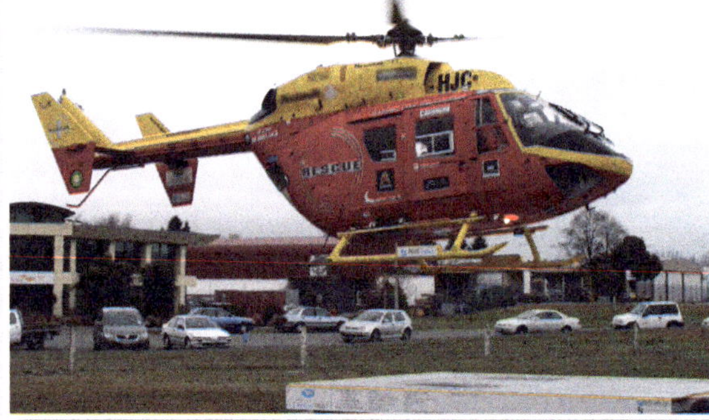

lifting up

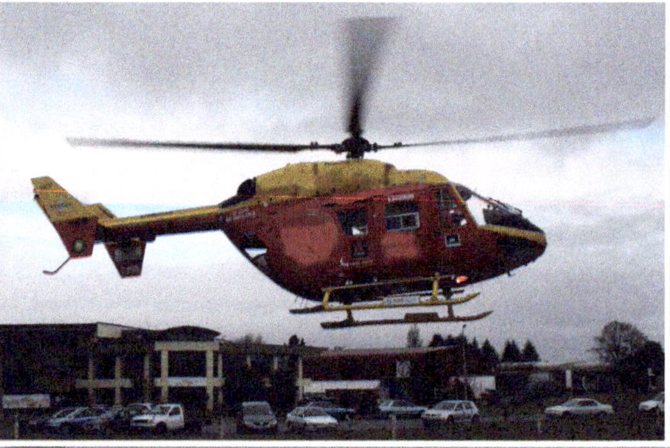

lifting off

Only Took Three Minutes!

Quentin lifts the helicopter a few metres off the ground. Then he turns it, and sweeps into the sky.

I check my watch. It's only been three minutes since the emergency call.

Someone, somewhere, will soon be very happy to see and hear the helicopter "Hotel Juliet Charlie". Quentin and Wayne are coming to the rescue!

ready to rescue

"Hotel Juliet Charlie" on its way

Index

Glossary

airspace	The area of the sky where aircraft regularly fly
hangar	A large building that houses aircraft, such as helicopters
pagers	Electronic messaging devices that alert people when there is an urgent call
paramedics	Medical professionals who give medical treatment to patients before they get to hospital
revolutions	The number of times something, like a rotor, spins around
rotors	The large blades that spin above a helicopter, enabling it to fly
throttle	The control that allows a pilot to increase or decrease the speed of an engine
winching	Using a wire rope attached to a machine to raise or lower heavy loads